TOMBSTONE JACK AND THE WYOMING RAIDERS

Also by Dan Winchester

TOMBSTONE JACK AND THE WYOMING RAIDERS

Dan Winchester

Denton & White
2018

WES
Winchest

Tombstone Jack and the Wyoming Raiders
©2018 by Gary Jonas

Any similarity to anyone living or dead is a coincidence, and if you say otherwise, you must be off your rocker, so don't go there. The author made it up.

This edition published by Denton & White

January 2018

ISBN-13: 978-1983537318
ISBN-10: 1983537314

CHAPTER ONE

Gus Nelson stood over the last survivor and laughed. The young woman beneath him didn't have the breath to scream, and even if she did, it wouldn't matter because the only person close enough to hear was Nelson's man, Mondo.

The woman, Bridget Decker, looked over at her husband, Horace. His body draped backward over a broken wagon wheel, his glassy, sightless eyes open, arms hanging outward, with a single bullet hole in the center of his forehead. The driver lay on the ground a few feet away, multiple bullet holes in his back. Their Conestoga wagon lay on its side, canvas flapping in the soft wind. Their belongings were strewn about on the ground. Bridget had planned to start a new life in Cheyenne. Women could vote in the Wyoming Territory. Women could serve on juries, as bailiffs, and even as the justice of the peace. Now Bridget knew that she would never get to do any of those things. She knew she'd draw her last breath in the middle of nowhere.

Gus Nelson kept laughing and waving his gun around. Bridget rolled over and tried to crawl away, but he kicked her in the back of the head, driving her face into the dirt beside the broken wagon.

"Where do you think you're going?" he asked.

She didn't reply.

"Check the men for money, and get the horses and the rest of the supplies loaded up," Gus said to his partner.

Mondo, a large hulking mountain of a man, climbed over the side of the wagon. "Supplies are all loaded, boss. Can I have the bitch?"

"Mondo, you need to back off," Gus said. "I'll get you a woman when we get to town, but you don't want this one."

"Why not?"

"Because she'll fight back."

"I like it when they fight back," he said taking the hat from Bridget's dead husband.

"Leave that hat alone!" Bridget yelled.

Mondo laughed. "You're right, Gus. She's still got some fight in her." He checked the hat. It was a nice Stetson known as a Boss of the Plains. "I like this." He put it on. "Bit small, but I'll make it work."

"Take that off!" Bridget said, pushing herself to her feet.

"Take it off me," Mondo said, leaning toward her. "I do love to play."

She rushed at him, but he caught her arms.

"Let's dance," he said and pulled her this way and that.

"Enough of this," Gus said. He pointed his gun at her and fired.

The bullet tore into her back.

Mondo jumped back, letting Bridget drop to her knees. "Dammit, Gus, you could have shot me!"

"But I didn't."

Bridget moaned in pain.

"Damn, boss, I was having fun."

Gus shot Bridget again and she fell forward, twitched once, and stopped moving.

"She's dead now," Gus said.

"I don't care if she's dead," Mondo said bending down to reach for her.

"No," Gus said. "Mr. Ryker gave us too much work to do. Sun will be going down soon, and there've been reports of Indians in the area."

"I scalp Indians for fun," Mondo said.

Gus shook his head. "I don't see the two of us taking on an entire tribe."

"You're the boss," Mondo said.

"Ryker's the boss," Gus said.

"Far as I'm concerned, you're the boss," Mondo said. "Mr. Ryker spends all his time reading those damn books."

"He's an edge-u-ma-cated man," Gus said, and they both laughed.

Mondo and Gus gathered supplies and checked the men's bodies for valuables.

Their mistake was not checking Bridget Decker's body for signs of life.

They set fire to the wagon, mounted their horses, and rode off into the distance. When they were gone, Bridget crawled through the tall grass and rolled down into a gully. She was losing too much blood, and it was difficult to breathe, but she forced the air into her lungs. One way or another, she was going to find these men, and she was going to kill them.

CHAPTER TWO

"All's I'm saying is we should spend some time in a town for a while," Burt said. "Can't we go back to Cheyenne? It ain't that far away, and I think that girl, Sally, the dazzling blonde down at Madam West's, had a thing for me."

Burt was a thin man with a scraggly beard and a face that wore a constantly bewildered expression. He rode an old paint horse, and kept having to put a hand on his hat when the wind kicked up.

"Sally can wait," said Jack Coltrane. "Jess Chalker is in Pine Bluffs working a cattle herd, and he's worth two hundred dollars."

Jack rode a Morgan and wore a duster. He took off his hat and wiped his forehead as they rode up a slight inclined hill.

"I've been dreaming of Sally," Burt said. "Her soft blonde hair, her great big smile, her even bigger—"

"You see that?" Jack asked, pointing to a column of smoke a ways off on the plain.

"Fire," Burt said. "So?"

"Might be nothing," Jack said. "Might be something. Let's check it out."

"I'd rather go back to Cheyenne."

But Jack was already angling off toward the smoke on the horizon.

Burt sighed, and followed.

"Wait up!" Burt said.

Jack didn't hear him. The Morgan trotted toward the smoke, and as Jack grew closer, he saw it was a wagon still smoldering, but the flames were nearly out. A couple of dead men were sprawled on the ground. One of the corpses was blackened and cooked by the fire.

Jack raced over, dismounted and checked the men. They were dead.

Burt caught up, and climbed off his horse. "Indians?" Burt asked.

Jack shook his head. "Robbers." He spotted blood on the grass. He knelt and looked around. Unless one of the robbers was shot, or one of the dead men moved, this was another victim.

There was more blood a few feet away. Jack followed the trail, and it led him through the tall grass to a gully.

A woman lay face down in the narrow ravine. She'd been shot in the back. Twice.

Jack raced down the embankment and knelt beside her. She was still breathing.

"Burt!" Jack called.

Burt appeared at the top of the gully. His eyes widened. "Holy smokes! Is she…"

"She's alive," Jack said. "But she's been shot. She needs a doctor."

"Closest one will be back in Cheyenne."

"Old Jess will have to wait," Jack said. "I can't leave a woman out here to die."

He did what he could to staunch the bleeding.

"She ain't gonna make it," Burt said. "She's lost too much blood."

Jack knew Burt was probably right, but it didn't matter. "As long as she's breathing, I'll do what I can to make sure she survives."

Burt looked around at the bodies and the burned out wagon. "What about these men? Ain't right to just leave 'em."

"Give them a proper burial. I'll see you back in town."

"But…" A gust of wind took Burt's hat off his head. He chased after it.

By the time he snatched the hat from the tall grass, and plopped it back on his head, Jack was already in the saddle, holding the woman in front of him. He kicked his horse into motion, and they rode off toward Cheyenne.

Burt shook his head. "Sure," he said. "I'll stay back here and bury the dead all by my lonesome. Don't mention it, Jack. And if the killers come back, I guess they'll shoot me, too. Thank you very much."

Jack was too far away to hear his friend. He held the woman, and urged his horse to go faster. Liquid warmth soaked through his shirt.

"Hold on, ma'am," he whispered into the woman's ear. "I've got you."

Jack had seen too much senseless death to be a religious man. He'd killed too many men to think he was a righteous man, though everyone he killed certainly deserved it. That didn't make him a good man. It just meant he was a man who found himself in bad situations, and most of the time, as a bounty hunter, he sought out those situations for financial gain.

But innocent people were to be protected.

Some men needed killing.

Hell, some women deserved it, too.

People could be cold and vicious.

Jack could get right down in the mud with them, but he tried not to be cruel about it. He didn't mind killing, but he also didn't mind *not* killing. It was a question of honor.

The woman had run into men with no honor. That was unfortunate. Two men were dead. Jack had seen worse, and normally, he didn't let his thoughts wander this territory because life in the west was always tough. The land itself tried to kill you. But the people who came west were also tough. This woman looked too soft to be out here. She felt too small and frail.

But she was clearly a fighter. She kept drawing breath.

The strong were honor bound to protect the weak. That's how civilization worked. If the weak died, that was a shame, but it wasn't something you just stood by and watched.

"You keep on breathing," Jack whispered. "You're not going to die today. Not on my watch."

CHAPTER THREE

The wind carried the ripe odors of Cheyenne across the plains, so before Jack rode past the frame houses, shanties, and rubbish heaps to get to the main street, he'd been breathing the fumes of animal dung and refuse.

The town itself was drab. Dead grass, burned brown by the sun, stuck out in patches from the dirt. Wind blew dust across the flat land.

As Jack rode past the various saloons and gambling halls, music poured into the street. In front of one saloon, a man sat in a chair with a violin doing a terrible rendition of "Shoo Fly, Don't Bother Me."

Jack wished the man wouldn't bother people with his warbling.

The sun was sinking as Jack dismounted and carried the injured woman into the doctor's office.

An older gentleman in a white shirt and black trousers met him in the front room. He hooked his thumbs into his suspenders and snapped them, then motioned toward a long table.

"She's been shot," Jack said.

The old man nodded. "I can see that."

"What can I do to help?" Jack asked.

The man whistled, and shrugged. He walked around the table, examining the woman. He checked the bullet holes in her back then placed a hand on her face.

"Caroline?" he called.

From deeper in the building a woman's voice responded. "Coming, Frank. Don't get your knickers twisted."

Frank frowned and looked at Jack. "This your wife?" he asked.

Jack explained the situation.

Frank frowned.

"I'll cover any costs, Doc," Jack said, and placed some money on a counter.

"I ain't the doctor," Frank said. "Caroline is."

An old woman came through the back doorway into the office. "What do we have?" she asked.

"Hello, Caroline," Frank said. "You have a patient. Two gunshot wounds to the back. Pretty bad."

Caroline checked the injured woman then barked orders and Frank jumped into action. She glared at Jack. "You," she said. "Out." And she pointed to the main door.

The old man gave Jack a shrug. "She's in charge here. I just help out."

Jack nodded. He didn't care who took care of the woman. He just wanted her to survive. "I'll be in the saloon across the street."

Frank shook his head, and cocked a thumb to the right. "Go to the one three doors down. McDaniels. Less trouble there. Better whiskey, too."

"Much obliged," Jack said and moved toward the door.

"Hey," Caroline said as she worked to get the woman's dress cut open. "I'll send Frank over to update you once she's out of the woods. What's your name?"

"Appreciate it," Jack said. "And my name's Jack Coltrane."

He stepped out onto the sidewalk and checked on his horse. He untied it from the post and walked it down the street.

A clothing store next to the doctor's office had a huge plate glass window that acted like a mirror. Jack glanced at his reflection. He frowned and looked down at his shirt, opening his duster a bit. Sure enough, two large splashes of red stained the material. He looked like he'd been gut-shot.

He shrugged. He'd looked worse.

The saloon was slow in the early evening. A few men played a game that looked similar to faro while a few others nursed whiskeys at the bar, and a bartender wiped a ubiquitous glass that would likely never get any cleaner.

Jack took a seat at the bar away from the other men. The bartender walked down to him. "You bleeding?" the bartender asked.

Jack glanced down at his shirt. "Not my blood," he said.

The bartender nodded, and if he had any desire to know the rest of the story, it never reached his eyes. "What'll it be?" he asked.

"Whiskey," Jack said.

The bartender nodded again, this time with approval. He set the glass he'd been cleaning on the counter, took a bottle of whiskey from the shelf behind him, and poured a healthy shot. He slid the glass to Jack, who tossed some money on the counter.

A slow swipe of the hand, and the bartender made the money disappear. "Enjoy," he said.

Jack nodded his thanks and sipped his drink.

A few minutes later, two men entered the saloon, and grabbed a table. One of them was large and held a perpetual frown on his face like the world had made a joke at his expense and wouldn't stop telling it to every single person in town. The other man's eyes swept the room and settled on Jack for a moment, sizing him up. When Jack didn't react to the appraisal, the man took a seat. "Perry," he said. "Bring us some whiskey."

The bartender grabbed two glasses and filled them. He pushed the glasses toward the two men at the other end of the bar from Jack. The men ignored the glasses and turned to look at the new entrants. One of the men was slender while the other looked like he'd won the pie-eating contest in every county for the last thirty years running.

"Gus," the skinny man said. "You and Mondo is late."

"Mondo and I are right on time. Bring us the whiskeys, Perry. I ain't gonna ask again."

The heavier man turned on his barstool. "You have yet to ask, and Perry here happens to be correct. You and Mondo are late."

Gus winked at him. "Perry said *is*. You'd think spending his time around you and Mr. Ryker, he'd soak up some book learning."

"If you want your whiskey, you can come and retrieve it yourself."

"Now, now, Victor. Don't get yourself all worked up. Maybe you should bring those glasses over here to us your own self. You could sure use some exercise."

"Fellas," the bartender said, "I don't want any trouble in here."

Victor stood, turned, and faced Gus and Mondo. "You will show me some respect, Gus Nelson."

Gus leaned back in his chair. "Or what?"

"Or you and I will settle this like men out in the street."

Gus laughed. "You'd have a heart attack just trying to walk out to the street. Maybe we should settle it right here, right now."

Perry grabbed the whiskey glasses from the counter and rushed over to the table with them. "No need for no one to get shot up, Gus. I got your drinks right here, I do."

Perry set the drinks on the table and positioned himself between Gus and Victor.

"Much obliged, Perry," Gus said with a grin. "I do declare, you just saved old Victor's life. He ought to thank you for that because I was just about to fill his heart with lead."

Victor took a step forward, but Perry turned and pushed him back to the barstool.

"Let it go," Perry said. "It ain't worth it."

Jack watched the exchange, then threw back his whiskey in one gulp. He set the glass on the counter a little louder than necessary, and everyone turned to look at him. He pointed at the bartender, then to his glass.

The bartender walked over to give him a refill.

"You might want to keep it down, Stranger," Gus said.

Jack took a sip of whiskey.

Gus laughed. "That's what I thought you said."

Mondo turned to look at Jack, then back to Gus. "I want to fight that man," Mondo said.

"Some other time," Gus said. "We have whiskey to drink. And I think Victor and Perry want to join us at our table to talk business."

"We work for Mr. Ryker, not for you," Victor said.

"You hardly work *with* us, Victor. I'm tired of you not pulling your own weight in the outfit, though I admit it would take a hell of a lot of effort."

"You ain't funny," Perry said.

"Sit down, Twig," Gus said.

Perry sat on the stool.

"Not there, Twig," Gus said. He kicked a chair out from the table. The chair made a scraping noise then tipped backward a bit before settling on all four legs again. "I told you to join us."

Perry hesitated, but crossed the floor to the chair. As he moved, he said,

"Mr. Ryker ain't gonna be happy if he hears about you treating us bad."

"Who's gonna tell him?" Gus asked and laughed. He turned to Mondo. "Hey, Mondo, are you gonna tell Mr. Ryker I was mean to these two idiots?"

"Nope," Mondo said.

Gus pounded on the table, nearly spilling his whiskey. "How about you, Victor? You gonna tell Mr. Ryker about this?"

"No," Victor said.

"Well, I know I ain't gonna tell him." Gus leaned forward and patted Perry on the knee. "That leaves you."

Perry trembled as Gus smiled at him.

Gus pulled his gun and shoved it up under Perry's chin. "Are you gonna tell him?" Gus asked, his voice calm.

Perry tried to lean away from the gun, but Gus kept the pressure on, shoving the barrel into the soft flesh above his throat. Perry whimpered.

"I didn't hear you," Gus said, cocking the hammer back. "Speak up."

"Leave him alone," Victor said. "He's not going to tell."

"I need to hear it from him," Gus said.

"I ain't gonna tell no one," Perry said.

"What about you, Joe?" Gus asked.

The bartender shook his head. "What's said in here, stays in here," the bartender said.

"What about you, Stranger?" Gus asked Jack. "I see you eyeballing me. You got something to say?"

Jack didn't bother to look over. "Shut up and drink your whiskey."

"You telling me what to do?" Gus asked, rising from his chair, gun still cocked.

Jack sighed. He got up from his chair and walked to the table where Gus stood. He snatched the revolver from Gus's hand, and smacked the son of a bitch in the nose with the butt of the gun. Gus stumbled backward and fell on his ass. His hand went to his nose. Blood trickled between his fingers.

Mondo started to push himself up, but Jack shoved him back in his chair so hard, Mondo tipped over and smacked his head on the floor.

Jack released the cylinder, dumped the bullets on the now seated Gus. He slapped the cylinder back in place then placed the gun on the table. He stared down at Gus.

"Get up when you're good and ready. Then sit down, shut up, and drink your damn whiskey," Jack said.

Mondo was on his hands and knees now. Jack helped the big man up and stared into his eyes. "Your friend starts any more trouble, I'm taking my bad day out on you. Got it?"

Mondo was a large man, and while he wasn't the brightest, he recognized that Jack was not someone he wanted "taking out a bad day" on him. He nodded.

Jack returned to the bar. He tossed back his drink, pointed to his glass. "Refill, bartender, and Gus over there has agreed to pay for it."

"Yes, sir," the bartender said.

Gus got up, and bullets clattered to the floor around him. He snatched his gun off the table, threw an angry glare at Jack, then stormed out of the saloon.

The bartender grinned. "I'll put it on his tab."

CHAPTER FOUR

The saloon's business picked up within a few hours. The tables filled, men bellied up to the bar and ordered whiskeys, a red-headed singer in a blue dress took up a spot beside a piano and a balding man sat down to tickle the eighty-eights. The woman started singing, and some people paid attention, though most stuck to their conversations or card games.

Jack liked the way the woman sang. Her voice reminded him of simpler times. Not that times were ever that simple, but there were a few months before he went off to war when he was young and in love with a woman named Eliza. The singer's soft voice took him back to those months, and he wondered what trails his life could have gone down if the war hadn't interrupted.

He never saw Eliza after the war. Sometimes he wondered what happened to her. Had she married? Did she have kids? Was she still alive? What would she think of the man he'd become?

Would she approve of the killing? Would his skill with the guns and his fists scare her? Would she embrace the person he'd become or would she shy away from him? Eliza had been a calm spot in his life, and sometimes he sought refuge in his memory of her. The nights spent in her arms, talking about a life together that would never happen, laughing about the times they might have shared had things not taken a different turn.

He'd killed one man before he met her—his own father. That night haunted him, but she made the nightmares go away.

He killed many more men in the war. He was good at it. Some of those faces came to him in dreams, but war was different. It was kill or be killed. And when it came down to it, Jack was very good at killing, so after the war, he rode west and hunted bad men down. Some of those men caught bullets from Jack's guns. Some of them were simply turned in to local sheriffs.

The killing didn't bother Jack. The men he killed had it coming. If they hadn't been bad men, they wouldn't have found themselves on the wrong end of his Colts.

He sipped his whiskey and shook his head. The booze was getting to him, sending him down the dark alleys of his soul, and the singer kept bringing up images of Eliza.

He tossed back the rest of his whiskey, and was going to order another, but Frank cut through the crowd and found him at the bar.

"Mr. Coltrane," he said, leaning against the bar near Jack. "The woman is going to live. Caroline patched her up and she's sleeping now."

Frank pushed some money at Jack, who looked a question at him.

"You left too much money," Frank said.

Jack nodded and tucked the money into his pocket. "Has the woman regained consciousness?"

Frank shook his head. "Not yet, but Caroline says she's tough. You saved the woman's life, Mr. Coltrane."

"It was the right thing to do," Jack said.

"There's a nice hotel half a block down. If you get a room there, I'd be happy to let you know when she rouses. I expect she'd like to meet the man who saved her."

Jack shrugged. He didn't know about that. He had to get to Pine Bluffs to collect Jess Chalker.

"I think it would mean a lot to her," Frank said. "I know if it were me, I'd want to be able to say thanks."

"I'll take that into consideration," Jack said. "But I have a job to do and it's not in Cheyenne."

"I suspect it can wait," Frank said. "No offense, Mr. Coltrane, but I know who you are."

Jack turned his head and met Frank's gaze.

Frank put up his hands. "You don't remember me, but a few years back, I was a deputy here. You brought in a man name of Carter Bishop. Sheriff had me get your money wired. I also took Mr. Bishop to Caroline."

Jack remembered Carter Bishop. The man fancied himself a gunfighter. The man overestimated his skill.

"So Caroline is one for two," Jack said and studied Frank. "I do remember you, Frank. You made sure I got the full reward."

"Well, Bishop was still alive when you brought him in," Frank said.

Jack nodded.

"Bishop was well-known in outlaw circles," Frank said. "Word is that his death is what earned you the nickname Tombstone Jack. Is that true?"

"If you say so," Jack said.

He'd actually picked up the nickname in Arizona when he rode with a posse, and it had nothing to do with bringing people in dead, it had everything to do with there being two men named Jack in the group, and as Jack had come in from Tombstone, that became his extra moniker. But the name tended to put some fear into the hearts of outlaws, and Jack kinda liked for them to be afraid of him. They were less likely to fight because they knew he'd kill them.

Jack looked over as Burt entered the saloon.

Burt scanned the crowd, spotted Jack and Frank talking at the bar, and snaked his way through the people to join them.

"I hate burying folks," Burt said.

"Burt," Jack said, "this is Frank. He works with the doctor who saved the woman we found this morning. And Frank, this is Burt. He travels with me."

"And it looks like he needs a drink," Frank said.

"You can say that again," Burt said.

"No need," Frank said. "Your first drink is on me."

Frank motioned to the bartender, and paid for Burt's whiskey.

"Refill?" the bartender asked Jack while he had the bottle out.

Jack shook his head. "I'm good."

The bartender shoved a glass of whiskey to Burt, then moved down to take care of his other customers.

Burt raised his glass to Frank. "You're my new best friend, good sir."

Frank laughed. "One can't have too many friends."

CHAPTER FIVE

Against Jack's better judgment, he and Burt dropped by the doctor's office the next morning. Jack wanted to simply head to Pine Bluffs, but Burt insisted it would be rude to leave town without checking on the woman they'd found.

"Frank won't be buying you more drinks," Jack said as they approached the doctor's office.

"I know that."

"Just making sure."

Frank opened the door and smiled. "Come on in, Jack, Burt," he said softly. "Bridget is awake, but keep your voices down because Caroline is still sleeping. She had a late night. Bad dreams."

"We'll be quiet," Burt whispered.

"You don't have to whisper, just keep your voices low and we should be fine and dandy."

"Lead on," Jack said, wanting to get this over with so he could hit the trail. He didn't think Jess Chalker was going anywhere, but he'd rather get to Pine Bluffs, collect the man, and turn him in for the reward sooner than later.

Frank led the way to a back room where Bridget sat propped up against several feather pillows. She pulled the blankets up to cover her nightgown.

"Bridget," Frank said, "these are the men who saved you. Jack Coltrane brought you to our humble abode. And Burt here buried your husband and the driver."

"Howdy, ma'am," Burt said, taking off his hat.

Jack removed his hat and gave the woman a nod. "Pleasure to meet you," he said.

"Thank you," she said. She stared at them awkwardly.

Jack scuffed his feet. He had no idea what to say to her.

Burt held his hat and shrugged.

"I suppose I should thank you for bringing me to town," she finally said.

"You're welcome," Jack said.

"And for burying my husband," she said, looking to Burt.

"Least I could do. Sorry for your loss."

"My husband was murdered," Bridget said, raising her voice. "So was Mr. Timmons, the driver."

"Yes, well," Frank said, motioning her to keep her voice down. "My wife is sleeping and she's a bearcat if she ain't sawed enough logs."

"We'll get out of your hair," Jack said. He glanced at Bridget. "I hope you heal up right quick."

She stared at him for a moment, her eyes going to his waist and down to his thigh where his holster was tied off. "I don't see a badge," she said.

"I'm not a lawman," Jack said.

"But one look in your eyes tells me you've killed men."

"I was in the war."

"Of course. May I have a word with you in private, Mr. Coltrane?"

"We can wait outside," Burt said.

"Yes, we can do that," Frank said.

He and Burt left the room. Jack stood next to the doorway, hat in hand.

"Are you good with that gun?" she asked.

"I know which end to point where," Jack said.

"I know the names of the men who shot me, and killed my husband and driver."

"That might be something you should take up with the sheriff."

"I did. He was here an hour ago."

"I don't follow," Jack said.

"He refused to believe me. A man named Gus Nelson killed my husband. His henchman, big man named Mondo, killed Mr. Timmons. Gus shot me, too. They took what they wanted and left us there to rot." Her voice rose with the last statement.

Jack drew a deep breath as he thought about his meeting with Gus and Mondo the previous night. He motioned with his palm down. "I'm right here," he said. "I can hear you."

"Are you afraid of Caroline?" she asked.

"Can't say as I am, but I try not to upset folks who can dig bullets out of me and patch me up."

"You get shot a lot, do you?"

"Time to time."

"It hurts," Bridget said.

Jack nodded. "Sure does."

"Caroline says I have a broken rib to go along with the bullet wounds. If I could move, I'd go door to door to find Gus Nelson and put a bullet in him. Since I can't do that right now, I was hoping maybe you could."

"I have a job to handle in Pine Bluffs."

"How long will that take?"

"Few days."

"Can you come back after that? Gus Nelson needs to pay for what he did."

"What did the sheriff say?"

"Gus is the sheriff's cousin. Sheriff said Gus would never shoot a woman. Obviously, he's lying because here I am, all shot up. I have money. My husband wired some ahead of us so we'd have it waiting here."

Jack scratched his head. "You and me, we just met, so I think maybe you misjudged me."

"You kill people for money, Mr. Coltrane. I know your job in Pine Bluffs is bringing in a wanted man. You're a bounty hunter. They call you Tombstone Jack."

Jack sighed and looked behind him at the doorway. He frowned and looked back at Bridget. "Frank told you that, did he?"

"Not directly. He came in drunk last night and bragged about you to Caroline."

"As far as I know, there are no papers sworn out on Mr. Nelson. If I go put a bullet in him for you, that makes me a common murderer. That's the kind of man I hunt down and bring to justice. You see the dilemma," he said, not making it into a question.

"You don't want to hunt yourself down, but you never let a man get away."

Jack couldn't help but grin. "I'm not a hired gun."

"Can you at least check to see if Gus Nelson is wanted? He stole our horses, too."

"Not much worse than a horse thief," Jack said.

"Will you please check? You saved my life, so you're responsible for my safety. Isn't that how these things work?"

"I wouldn't know."

"Then that's exactly how these things work. Unless you think it's right for a man to shoot a woman."

"Depends on the circumstances," Jack said.

"Well I never!"

"Shh," Jack said. "Doctor lady is sleeping."

"You're an irritating man."

"Thank you, ma'am," Jack said, and turned to leave.

"I did nothing to him," Bridget said. "We were riding to Cheyenne to start a new life. Horace was going to open a mercantile store. We were going to start a family. Gus Nelson and his henchman took that away from us. The sheriff doesn't care. And you don't care either."

"If I didn't care, I'd have left you out on the plains to die."

"Then help me get justice."

Jack turned to face her once more. "You just rest easy and heal up." He gave her another nod, put on his hat and walked out.

CHAPTER SIX

"Burt, go get the horses," Jack said as he stepped out of the doctor's office. "I'm going to go talk to the sheriff."

"You got it," Burt said. "I'll meet you there."

Jack strode down the street to the sheriff's office. He pushed open the door and stepped inside.

The sheriff, a tall, rugged man with a thick mustache and beard sat at a desk reading the newspaper. A deputy stepped out of the hallway that led to the cells, and hung a ring of keys on a nail next to the door.

"Howdy," the deputy said. "Can I help you?"

"I'm here to talk to the sheriff," Jack said.

The sheriff looked up from the paper. "That would be me," he said, and closed the paper. "Sheriff Dawkins. What can I do for you?"

"Do you know a man named Gus Nelson?" Jack asked.

Sheriff Dawkins studied him. "Who's asking?"

"Interested citizen," Jack said.

"What's your name?"

"Jack."

"Well, Jack, you're the second person today to ask me about my cousin. What's your interest?"

"Word on the street is he's a horse thief and a killer. Man like that is bound to be wanted somewhere."

"Strong accusations," Sheriff Dawkins said. "But ol' Gus ain't like that. He's a wanted man, but mostly by Tanya Welker, the local seamstress.

She's been pining after my cousin since she was twelve years old."

"Millie Doherty's been pining for him, too," the deputy said with a smile. "Gus fancies himself a ladies man, and the ladies back him up on that."

"Can't say as he impressed me much," Jack said.

"So you've met him?" the deputy asked.

"We weren't formally introduced, but he'll remember me."

"Maybe you shouldn't ought to rush to judgment."

Jack grinned. "Men like him often have legal problems."

"Not Gus," Sheriff Dawkins said.

"Because you sweep his problems out the door?" Jack asked.

"Now, I know you don't mean that to sound like an insult."

Jack grinned. "Then you might want to clean out your ears, Sheriff."

Sheriff Dawkins pushed himself to his feet and walked around the desk. He stepped right up, and stared up into Jack's eyes. "I don't cotton to threats, Jack."

"I haven't threatened you, Sheriff. I simply questioned your professionalism."

Dawkins glared up at Jack. "I think it's time you left my office. And if you know what's good for you, you'll leave my town."

"Sheriff Dawkins," Jack said, staring down at him. "If you know of any warrants for Gus or his friend Mondo, you're duty-bound to tell me."

"I'm duty-bound to throw you out of town. I don't cotton to bounty hunters, either."

The deputy stepped forward, but the sheriff held up a hand.

"It's all right, David. Jack here was just leaving. He don't want no trouble with the law here." He intensified his glare at Jack. "Ain't that right, Jack?"

Jack held his gaze. "Trouble comes in on the wind all the time," Jack said. He licked a finger and held it up. "I don't feel a gust yet, but the day is young." He glanced at the deputy then back to the sheriff. "You have a nice day now, you hear?"

And he left the office.

Burt rode up with Jack's horse in tow. Jack walked over and took the reins. He put a foot in the stirrup, and swung his leg over the saddle.

"Everything okay?" Burt asked.

"Probably not." Jack nudged his horse to trot down the street.

CHAPTER SEVEN

Jack rode out of town with Burt by his side. "We'll go catch Jess Chalker in Pine Bluffs, collect the reward, then swing back by Cheyenne to check on Mrs. Decker."

A gust of wind nearly took Burt's hat. He caught the hat and pulled it down on his head. "One of these days, I need to get a new hat."

"You do seem to spend a lot of time chasing the one you've got."

"It hates me," Burt said.

"Why did you buy it when it didn't fit?"

"I didn't buy it," Burt said. "Miss Angela gave it to me in El Paso. She was a sight to see. Anyway, I keep it to remember her by. She's like my guardian angel."

"How so?" Jack asked, happy to have mindless conversation on the trail.

"Because this hat has saved my life. Not once, but twice."

"Do tell."

"First was when an Indian fella threw a knife at me, but my hat fell off, so I bent over to get it and the knife went right over me."

"What happened to the Indian?"

"Nothing. He was drunk and thought I was someone else. So I let it go. I mean, I ain't big like you, so I tend to let a lot of things go."

Jack shrugged. Burt wasn't the bravest man around, but he was good company. He could cook. He didn't mind keeping watch. He was mostly in a good mood. And he'd warned Jack of danger more than a few times.

"And the hat saved you again?"

"Yeah," Burt said. "I was trying to make it to a stagecoach, but the wind whipped my damn hat away. I went chasing after it and it landed in the mud, so I decided to go clean it off. By the time I got back, the coach had left without me."

"I trust something happened to the coach?"

Burt nodded. "Sure did. Bandits. Them sumbitches gunned down all the folks in the coach."

"Could be a coincidence."

"Once, maybe. But twice?"

"So you think the ghost of Miss Angela is watching over you?"

"That's stupid," Burt said. "Miss Angela is still alive. She works for Madame Torgeson."

"So you just think it's a lucky hat."

"I was lucky Miss Angela gave it to me. I was lucky to spend some time with her."

"And how much did that time cost you?"

"That ain't important. She could have said no. And she knew the hat was lucky because she said so when she gave it to me."

Jack laughed. "Or maybe her previous customer forgot his hat, and she didn't want it taking up space in her room."

"Either way," Burt said, "it's my lucky hat, and while I might cuss it a few times when it flies off, I ain't about to replace it."

They rode for a while.

Jack turned to Burt. "Was Miss Angela the redhead?"

"As a matter of fact, she was."

"You know, I seem to recall losing a hat the last time I paid her a visit," Jack said.

Burt glared at him. "You're just messing with me."

"That's true. I would never wear a hat like that. Too lady-like."

"You're just jealous that Miss Angela gave me a lucky hat."

Jack laughed again. "You're just upset that she charges you."

"She charges everyone. She's a whore."

"She's never charged me a red cent," Jack said.

"You ain't never been with her."

Jack gave him a wink. "You go on believing that."

CHAPTER EIGHT

Jess Chalker was one of the cowboys working for a rancher just outside Pine Bluffs. When Jack and Burt rode up to the main house, the rancher was out on his porch in a rocking chair. The man's name was Elmore Doherty, and his spread held cattle, horses, chickens, and a couple of border collies that helped keep the other animals in line.

Elmore had a rugged face, white hair, and a big mustache that puffed out like a scared cat. He rose from his rocking chair when Jack dismounted in front of the house.

"You two looking for work?" Elmore asked. "I'm short a couple of men, and I need some horses broke."

"You're about to be short one more man," Jack said and pulled a wanted poster from his pocket, unfolding it as he walked to the porch.

Burt remained in the saddle, keeping watch behind him.

Elmore accepted the poster. "Chalker," he said, rubbing his chin. "Figures. He's one of the hardest workers, and I had plans for him. He's in the back forty tending to the herd."

"Much obliged," Jack said.

Elmore studied the paper. "Says here he's wanted for forgery. Chalker can't write his own name. Ain't no way he's a forger."

"They can determine that after I turn him in."

"Maybe we can work something out. My granddaughter is sweet on him. Be a shame if he had to go to jail for crimes he didn't even commit."

"I fetch them," Jack said. "I don't try them."

"But your main goal is just to get paid. Ain't that right?"

"That is the end goal," Jack said.

"Then we should have a little chat. You men look like you could use some coffee. Come on inside. I'll have Nellie brew some up."

Jack shook his head. He opened his mouth to decline. "I think we—"

"It ain't like Chalker's going anyplace. He'll be back at the big house in a few hours anyway. Gives us time to talk. I'd appreciate it if you'd accept my hospitality. We have biscuits."

Jack gave in. "Well, I do like biscuits. Fine. We'll join you for a spell. Come on, Burt."

Burt hopped down. He tied their horses to a post, and they followed Elmore inside.

The ranch house was well-furnished with imports from around the world. As they walked through the house, Elmore waved at the rooms. "My late wife, God rest her soul, had a propensity for ordering stuff out of catalogues." He pointed at an odd post done up in onyx with stone branches shooting out from the top hooking up toward the ceiling. "I don't even know what that damn thing is. We use it as a coat rack."

Jack raised an eyebrow. He had no clue what its purpose might be either.

"Gertie ordered some of the strangest stuff, but she was my world. Been gone five years now, and I still miss her every day." He tossed an amused look Jack's way. "But I suspect old Mr. Caldwell at the General Store misses her more than I do. She darn near kept him in business all by her lonesome."

The kitchen had a small table off to one side. Elmore gestured to the chairs, then stepped outside onto the back porch to call out to Nellie.

He joined Jack and Burt at the table.

"Nice place you have here," Burt said. "Crowded, but comfy."

"That was all Gertie," Elmore said.

A moment later, the ugliest woman Jack had ever seen stepped into the house. She looked like she'd been tossed in the ugly forest to fight all the trees, and those trees sure got the best of her. One eye was lower than the other, and they looked off in opposite directions. Her nose was crooked as a casino dealer, and when she tried to smile, it was more like a grimace, and her mouth held two teeth—one on the top, one on the bottom, spaced out so they didn't even touch each other when she bit down. Her face was more pockmarked than the moon and her straggly hair looked like it was ready to jump off her head to run for cover. It went out in every direction. And those were her good points.

"Howdy, Nellie," Elmore said. "Can you whip up some coffee and biscuits for our guests."

"I sure can," Nellie said in a voice that sounded like a hawk choking on a rat.

Burt cringed.

Jack was more polite, but he tried not to look directly at her.

Elmore grinned and nodded.

Nellie poured them all cups of coffee and set a plate of biscuits in the center of the table.

"Want me to join you?" she asked.

"No, you go on outside," Elmore said.

"Thanks for the coffee and biscuits," Burt said, staring at the table.

"My pleasure," Nellie said.

Elmore lowered his voice to a conspiratorial whisper. "I keep her out back to scare the predators away."

"She ain't that bad," Burt lied.

"One of the hands said if she wanted to avoid getting raped, all she had to do was stand in the light."

"That's not nice," Burt said.

"Nice, no. True, yes."

Jack sipped some coffee. "What's your point?" he asked.

"Jess Chalker's in love with Nellie. And while that probably means he's blind in one eye and can't see out of the other, Nellie is forty-two years old and ain't never been kissed before Jess showed up."

"And?" Jack asked.

"And it's worth the price of the reward to have him stick around to marry her. What do you say? He's an innocent man. He ain't got the sense God gave to a dog, but he ain't a bad guy. Who else would marry my daughter?"

Burt glanced at Jack. "You ain't gonna say no to true love, are you?"

"Someone else is bound to track him down," Jack said.

"You're the third," Elmore said.

Jack laughed. "Your little spiel worked on the other men?"

"They felt sorry for Nellie. Poor girl needs a husband, and if Jess is hauled off to jail, what chance does she have? It ain't like he killed no one. And when he comes in here, I'd be happy to have him demonstrate his handwriting so's you know he ain't the guy they're really after."

"Forgery ain't as bad as killing," Burt said. "And if he's innocent, he don't deserve to go to jail."

Jack sighed. "Well, hell, it saves us the hassle of transport and collecting."

Elmore clapped his hands. "Thank you, good sirs. I'll ride into town with you and get some cash out of the bank."

Burt shook his head. "You don't gotta—"

Jack kicked Burt under the table. "What Burt is saying is that would be fine."

CHAPTER NINE

Mr. Ryder never got his hands dirty; he had his trusted men take care of things for him while he sat in one of his many rooms with his massive book collection. Gus Nelson and Mondo got the easy task of dealing with Bridget Decker. Victor and Perry got the more entertaining and difficult task of going after Tombstone Jack because Ryder wanted to test his sons.

Gus and Mondo were not happy about their assignment. As they rode from the ranch into town, Gus fumed, while Mondo didn't seem to care.

"We should be the ones going after that damn bounty hunter," Gus said.

"Ain't a big deal," Mondo said.

"Can't believe he asked my cousin about us."

"You're just mad that he embarrassed you."

"He took you down, too."

"He caught me by surprise. In a fair fight, I'd kill him."

"But why send Perry and Victor? Hell, Victor's horse might not survive the trip under all that weight. And Perry's gonna run away and piss his pants at the first sign of trouble."

Mondo shrugged. "They need to put on their big boy britches to prove themselves to their daddy. Stop thinking on it, Gus."

"I want to kill that son of a bitch myself. Maybe he'll kill Victor and Perry and we'll get another shot at him."

"Nah. Victor's a good shot with that rifle. That bounty hunter will be dead before he even knows he's in danger. Mr. Ryker knew you'd want him to know who killed him. Ain't no way he could send us for that very reason."

"I sometimes forget you can think things through," Gus said as they rode down the street to the doctor's office.

"I'm right, though, ain't I?"

"Yeah, I'd want him to know."

"That's why we're dealing with the woman. Mr. Ryker knows how you think."

"Well, one thing's for sure," Gus said as he dismounted. "That lady's gonna know who killed her."

"No harm in that."

Mondo slid out of his saddle and roped his horse to the post.

The two men didn't bother knocking. They kicked the front door open and stormed inside. The front room was empty, so they rushed into the back.

Bridget Decker sat up in her bed and screamed.

Frank bolted into the room with a rifle, but Gus shot him in the head before the old man could pull the trigger.

"Make sure the doctor lady doesn't come in here, but don't kill her. Mr. Ryker likes her."

Mondo nodded, and pushed into the next room. He spotted Caroline trying to climb out a window. He walked over, pulled her back inside, and spun her around.

"Nighty-night," he said and gave her a light punch in the eye. She staggered back, hit the large wooden bedpost, and fell to the floor. She didn't get up.

Mondo shrugged. He didn't think he hit her that hard, but she was an old lady, so maybe she just couldn't take a punch. He knelt and made sure she was still breathing.

Bridget Decker screamed bloody murder in the next room.

Mondo hurried back. He nearly tripped over Frank's corpse and watched Gus trying to tear Bridget's nightgown off.

"You're gonna give it up and you're gonna like it," Gus said.

Mondo frowned. "We ain't here for that," he said.

Gus shoved Bridget's head against the headboard, stunning her. He turned to look at Mondo. "And to think, last time you were the one who wanted her. You can have a go after I do."

Mondo shook his head. "Not after you've buttered the bun. Let's just kill her dead and go back to the ranch."

Bridget found her spirit and struggled again. Gus slapped her face, and threw himself on top of her. She tried to scratch him, but he caught her arms.

"I'm going to kill you!" Bridget screamed.

"Shut up," Gus said.

"You killed Horace and I'm going to kill you!"

She got a hand free and punched Gus in the throat. He gulped. She raised a knee into his crotch. He clutched his privates and pitched sideways. She kicked him off the bed and he hit the floor like a sack of potatoes.

"Ain't got time for this," Mondo said, then drew his pistol, and shot Bridget in the head.

Gus picked himself up, stared at the dead woman. "Dammit, Mondo!"

"You gonna have some fun now?" Mondo asked.

Gus shook his head. "Unlike you, I like them still breathing."

CHAPTER TEN

"That was a good thing you done," Burt said on the ride back to Cheyenne.

They'd stayed the night at Elmore's, but Jack hadn't bothered checking Jess's handwriting skills. It didn't matter. Jack felt he was doing right by Nellie, and he liked Elmore. Trusted him, too. Jess Chalker seemed to be enamored with the ugly woman, who smiled happily and rushed into the man's arms when she saw him. Jess proved his bravery by not running away. They spent a lot of time staring into each other's eyes. Well, Jess stared into one of Nellie's eyes. The other was taking in the doorway off to the left.

"You think Mrs. Decker's doing all right?" Burt asked as they rode along the trail.

"I hope so."

"She's easy on the eyes."

"No argument there," Jack said, scanning the horizon.

"Maybe you could win her heart and settle down."

"She just lost her husband," Jack said. "She's not going to be looking to replace him. And I'm not looking to settle down."

Burt grinned. "Lots of words from you there, Jack. Maybe you like her more than you think."

Jack reined in his horse. "Shh," he said.

Burt stopped his horse, too.

Jack looked around. He climbed off his horse, pulled his rifle, and motioned for Burt to get off the trail.

They were on a wide open plain, but there was a ridge about eight hundred yards away. It was the only break in the horizon.

"What is it?" Burt asked, keeping his voice low.

"Might be nothing, but I thought I saw a glint of sunlight by the ridge. Like the reflection off the glass in a rifle scope."

"That's gotta be eight hundred yards away. Ain't no way someone can shoot us from there with any accuracy."

"Depends on the rifle and the skill of the man using it. I knew a sharpshooter who claimed he could take out a man at twelve hundred yards with his Whitworth."

"You don't know him anymore? What happened?"

"Some woman's husband got home early and shot him at point blank range."

Jack leveled his rifle over the saddle and looked through the scope. It was a simple 4x Davidson, but it was sufficient. He spotted two men on the ridge. One held a rifle, but was busy talking to his partner and not looking through the scope.

"At least two men over there," Jack said.

"Think they're after us?"

"Not likely, but I'm not willing to chance it. Let's move off into the tall grass and back up over the hill and out of sight."

They led their horses into the grass, and headed over the hill. Jack kept his rifle in one hand, and made sure to keep his horse between himself and the men on the ridge.

"Keep going," Jack said.

A gust of wind took Burt's hat off, and Burt lunged back to snatch it out of the air.

Dirt popped off the ground in line with where Burt would have been, and a moment later, the crack of a rifle sounded.

"Move!" Jack shouted.

He and Burt raced toward the hill. Another gunshot sounded, but if it was aimed at them, it missed.

"There's no cover here," Jack said, scanning the area.

"What do we do?" Burt asked. "My lucky hat saved me again, but I don't want to count on it any more than I have to."

To his credit, Burt's voice didn't break, but Jack knew the man was afraid.

"I'll handle them," Jack said. "You take the horses. Ride like hell back to that ditch by the farm a mile back."

"Wait, what?"

"Just go," Jack said. "Find cover. Keep the horses safe. I'll come back for you once I deal with the shooters."

"Think they're just raiders? Or are they after us in particular?"

"Probably just raiders like those that killed Mrs. Decker's husband and driver. Some men get a taste for killing."

"That happens when they don't settle down," Burt said with a nod.

Jack grinned. "You got that right. Now take your lucky hat and go."

Burt hopped on his horse and rode, keeping the reins from Jack's horse in one hand. They tore off down the trail. Two more shots rang out, but they missed. Maybe Burt's hat really was lucky.

Jack ducked into the tall grass, kept himself low, and slowly moved toward the ridge, taking a long arc around to get there.

As he crawled through the grass, hoping any rustling would be mistaken for wind, his hand bumped into a big stick. It was time to test things. He pulled a knife from his boot, and stabbed it into the ground. He pulled the blade free, turned it and stabbed again to make an X. Then he jammed the stick into the intersection.

He moved a few feet away, took off his hat, and with a perfect fling, tossed the Stetson onto the stick.

A gunshot tore through the grass right beneath the hat.

Followed by another crack.

The stick shattered into splinters and the hat fell to the ground.

Jack kept low and moved away from the stick. He could come back for the hat once he took out the men who were trying to kill him.

He moved along, taking it slow and easy so as not to disturb the grass any more than necessary. It wouldn't be wise to leave too obvious a trail behind him. He knew he was doing well enough on that front because no bullets slammed into the ground.

The problem was that ahead of him, the grass thinned out, and if he wanted to get closer to the ridge, he'd be out in the open.

The men were good shots. Jack didn't stand a chance if he had to cross that open area.

He raised his rifle, sighted and slowly got to one knee, aiming toward the ridge. As he rose out of the grass, he planned to sweep the horizon for any movement, but luck was on his side.

A heavy man stood up and sighted along his rifle toward where Jack had used the stick and hat.

Jack saw him first, and smiled as he aimed for the man's head.

He squeezed the trigger.

The man's head snapped back, then he fell forward, dislodged a few rocks, and rolled down the embankment.

Jack stayed up to see if anyone else would try to spot him. Sure enough, a man poked his head above the ridge.

Jack fired.

The man ducked as a spray of dirt exploded into the air.

Jack rose and started walking toward the ridge. He swept his aim across the expanse in case the other man tried to spot him again.

As before, the man popped his head up to check out the situation. He wasn't in the same place, so Jack didn't get his shot off before the man ducked.

The other man hadn't moved. That didn't mean he was dead, though. Jack kept looking at him between sweeps of the top of the ridge just in case.

Jack reached the base of the incline, and from here, he could see that the prone man was dead with a bullet in the face. He recognized the man from the saloon, but couldn't recall his name.

Was it a coincidence? These men might be after him specifically, or they might just be raiders attacking any travelers. But Jack didn't like coincidences. He didn't trust them.

Knowing this was one of the two men who fetched drinks for Gus Nelson, the man who shot Bridget, told him all he really needed to know. He'd taken their measure in the bar, and the more capable man was already out of the fight. Jack glanced back at the field of tall grass beneath him, and saw he'd left more of a trail than he thought. Why hadn't they taken another shot?

"Your friend is dead," Jack called.

He heard the scuff of boots on dirt and rock.

"You looking to join him?" Jack asked, keeping his rifle trained on the area from which he'd heard the noise.

"No sir, I ain't," the man called back.

"All right, son. You can get through this alive. I know you're alone up there or someone else would have taken a shot at me. I've been out in the open for a while now. What's your name?"

"I ain't gotta tell you."

"That's true," Jack said. "But think of it this way. It's harder to shoot a man if you know his name. It humanizes him. Makes you think he's got family. My name is Jack."

"I already know your name," the man said.

Jack slowly crept up the ridge.

"Then you came after me specifically? That wasn't very bright. You should have brought more men."

"Who says I didn't? For all you know, they's sneaking up on you."

Jack laughed. "What's your name, kid?" He pushed his memory back to the saloon. "Barry? No, that's not right. Perry?"

"What's it to you?"

"It's more to you than it is to me, Perry. If I recall, you're a slender man who can't keep the fear from his eyes.

You kowtow to Gus and the mountain-size man."

"Mondo."

"That's right."

"Gus is gonna shoot you dead, Mister. And if he don't, Mondo's gonna stomp your brains out all over the ground."

"Meanwhile, you're sitting up there, back against a rock, trying not to piss yourself."

"Am not."

"Perry, let's make this easy. If I have to climb up there to get you, I'll put a bullet in your head like I did to your friend. What was his name?"

"Victor."

"Do you want to be dead like Victor here?"

"I stand up, you're gonna shoot me."

"I don't want to shoot you, kid. Give me a reason not to. Toss your guns over the side of the ridge, and stand with your hands up. You hear me, Perry? You do that, I promise I won't shoot you."

"I don't trust you."

"In that case, you'll have to stand up and try to shoot me before I can put a bullet in you. Think you can do that?"

"No."

"Then we're at an impasse, Perry. All right, I'm coming up, and if you don't get up now, I'll shoot you dead on account of you took some shots at me and my friend."

"Victor's the one who did the shooting. I can't shoot straight."

"Oh, I suspect you can shoot just fine, but you don't want to go that way with me. Last chance, Perry."

More shuffling.

"All right, I'm coming up now."

Jack started climbing, taking care to make noise.

"All right," Perry said. "I give up."

"Guns," Jack said.

Perry tossed two pistols and a Winchester rifle over the side of the ridge. The rifle slid to a stop against Victor's body. The pistols bounced a few times and landed in the grass.

Perry put his hands up and stood.

A gust of wind carried the smell of urine in Jack's direction. Perry had already wet himself.

Jack climbed up and towered over Perry. "I think it's time you answered some questions."

Perry dropped to his knees. "You gonna kill me?"

"That depends on you."

Perry gulped. "I don't wanna die."

"That means you'll be truthful. You and your friends are robbing travelers. Did you come after me?"

Perry hesitated.

"Don't lie to me, Perry," Jack said.

He sighed. "We was supposed to kill you."

"On whose orders?"

"Gus said it was Mr. Ryker's orders."

"I don't know Mr. Ryker."

"He runs the Wyoming Raiders."

"Never heard of them."

"Well, you have now."

"Incompetent outlaws." Jack pointed at the trail he'd left in the grass. "It was downright obvious where I was down there. Why didn't one of you shoot me? Were you afraid?"

"Victor said he got you. Saw your hat fly off and everything."

Jack shook his head. "Amateurs. How does Mr. Ryker know about me?"

"Gus and Mondo must have told him."

"Why?"

"Because you embarrassed them."

Jack considered that. He supposed it was possible, but he wasn't sure he bought it. He glanced at the sky. It was getting late. There would be time for more questions later.

"You have a shovel?" Jack asked.

"Small one in my pack. Why?"

"Because you need to bury your friend."

Perry shook his head. "He was my brother. He didn't deserve to die." He spoke the words like he expected Jack to apologize.

"A man shoots at me, he dies," Jack said. "No way around it."

"I didn't shoot at you," Perry said.

"That's why you're still breathing. Get your shovel."

"No offense to my brother, but digging a grave is more work than I can do. There's some rocks down yonder. Can't I just cover him up with those?"

"Doesn't matter to me. He's your brother."

CHAPTER ELEVEN

After Perry buried Victor with some rocks, Jack sent him out to retrieve his hat. He knew Perry wouldn't try to run because there was nowhere to run to, and because Jack remained on the ridge with his rifle.

Burt rode up a few minutes later, and they set up camp right there because it was getting late.

Burt cooked up some beans, while Jack sat on a rock and used a knife to clean beneath his fingernails. Perry sat on the ground, head down, and quiet.

"What's the lay of the land?" Burt asked.

"Perry here was mighty talkative. It's pretty simple. He, his brother Victor,

Gus, and the big guy, Mondo, all work for a man named Ryker. They go out and raid travelers throughout the area, and they even went so far as to give themselves a name. The Wyoming Raiders."

"Catchy," Burt said. "You want coffee with supper?"

"Of course."

Burt grabbed a canteen from his pack, and filled a pot with water. He moved the beans, and set the pot over the fire to heat up. "I'm guessing they attacked the Deckers, and then made the mistake of tussling with you."

"According to Perry, he and Victor were sent to kill us because we asked the sheriff about Gus Nelson. Says the final say was Mr. Ryker."

"It was," Perry said.

"I'm not so sure," Jack said.

"Why not?" Burt asked.

"Perry here is scared of Gus."

"And?"

"So scared he wouldn't tell Ryker that Gus was overstepping his bounds."

"I ain't a tattler," Perry said.

"You think Mr. Ryker is a schoolmarm?" Jack asked.

"He's always saying we should read books, but no, he ain't no schoolmarm."

"So there's something else going on. Gus and Mondo are holding out on Mr. Ryker, and you've been covering for them."

"What makes you say that?"

"Your reaction in the saloon. You promised not to tell. Why would Gus think you'd tell on him?"

Perry shrugged.

"Perry," Jack said, pointing his knife at the man. "I'm going to learn the truth one way or another. Do you want me to carve you up some, or do you just want to tell me?"

Perry swallowed hard.

Burt gave a slow turn to look at Jack, but didn't say anything.

"I'm not a patient man," Jack said, still pointing the knife.

"On account of my last name being Ryker."

Jack nodded, and put his knife away. "That explains why Ryker has you on the team. Is he your father or is he another brother?"

"Father."

Jack nodded. "One thing I can't figure."

"What's that?"

"How did you know where to find me?"

"Gus said you were in Pine Bluffs. I didn't ask how he knew."

"Damn," Jack said, and got to his feet. "Burt, you need to take Perry back to town on your own. After you feed him, feel free to tie him up so he doesn't run off."

"What are you doing?"

Jack went over to his horse. "I'm riding back tonight. Only one person in Cheyenne knew where we were heading."

"Bridget Decker," Burt said. "If Gus got hold of her, she's either a captive..."

Jack nodded, and climbed into the saddle. "Or she's dead."

CHAPTER TWELVE

Jack rode into Cheyenne at daybreak. The buildings told him nothing. Houses and shops hid the secrets of their occupants. Looking at the smoke rising from a chimney wouldn't tell you whether the husband inside beat his wife. It wouldn't tell you if a son or daughter had died from illness. It wouldn't tell you if the people inside were lawful or not.

As he rode past, he could look through the darkened windows of the buildings. Windows could provide a glance into the secrets. People might be gazing outside with a forlorn look, wishing they'd chosen another path in life. They might be reading by candlelight. They might be watching for intruders, worried about what the day might bring. Or they might just be sleeping, and trying to live life as best they could.

But the houses and windows kept their secrets to themselves as Jack dismounted in front of the doctor's office. He tied his horse to a hitching post, and walked up to knock on the door.

A few moments later, Caroline answered. She had a black eye and a noticeable limp as she stepped back to allow him entrance.

"You're too late," Caroline said, gesturing him inside.

Jack stepped across the threshold and followed Caroline into the next room.

"Undertaker will be by in a bit," she said.

Lying on the table were two bodies.

Frank and Bridget.

Each had been shot in the head.

"This was Gus Nelson's work?" Jack asked.

She nodded and stared at the floor. "And the big man, Mondo. He punched me so hard, I nearly passed out. When I could get up, I came in here to find Frank and Bridget dead."

"I'm sorry," Jack said.

"Wasn't your fault. There aren't any papers on Gus or Mondo."

"But there should be."

"Sheriff came by after they left. Told me he'd done all he could, and that I was lucky they need me to patch up their wounds from time to time."

She gazed at the dirty floor, focused on a dark spot of dried blood. She fought back tears.

"Where are they?" Jack asked.

"Sheriff rode out to Ryker's ranch."

"Deputies?"

She shook her head. "They look the other way, but none of them are involved with Ryker or the Wyoming Raiders."

"Will they help?"

"Ha!" she said.

"Fine. Where does Ryker live?"

She gave him directions to the ranch outside of town.

"I'm sorry about Frank and Bridget," Jack said, and turned to leave.

"You can't go out there alone. Ryker has forty men on his payroll."

"How many of them work as raiders?"

"Four main raiders, but sometimes others ride with them to help gather up the take."

"So most of the men are just hands working the ranch. That's all I need to know."

She didn't say anything as he walked out of the office.

Jack untied his horse. He looked up and down the street at the buildings. People were just getting up to start their day. Ryker's men probably didn't have any tangible effect on their lives. These people minded their own business. Many of them likely never had any reason to interact with Ryker or his raiders.

Jack patted his horse. There weren't any papers on these men. Going after them might be the right thing to do, but the law would look at it as murder.

And in this case, the law was in on it.

Jack felt responsible for Bridget and Frank. If he hadn't left town to do the job in Pine Bluffs, he'd have been here to protect them.

It was time to end this. Jack mounted up and rode off toward the Ryker ranch.

CHAPTER THIRTEEN

It was mid-morning when Jack crested a small hill and gazed down at the spread where Ryker lived. He didn't waste any time. He simply rode down the trail to the main house, ignoring the ranch hands' quarters. Horses were penned up on the right, while an empty pen stood nearby. A barn stood in the center, and the big house was off to the left a ways. Beyond that was a working farm.

Two men led a horse from one round pen to the other.

Jack rode up to them. "Howdy," Jack said. "Mr. Ryker here?"

One man pointed to the house. "He's in there with the sheriff, sir."

"Much obliged." Jack tipped his hat to the men.

"Want us to take care of your horse?"

Jack shook his head. "No need. I won't be here long."

"Ain't no bother. We got oats and water in pails right over there. Looks like a fine Morgan."

"He is," Jack said. "You men worked here long?"

"No, sir. We hired on last week to help break some horses. Ryker's team brought in a beautiful herd a while back."

Jack considered things. "On second thought, my horse could use some food and water. Can you keep him out here, though?"

"Yes, sir."

Jack dismounted and patted the horse. "How many hands are working here today?"

"Quite a few. Most are out tending the fields, building a fence on the south forty, or taking care of the animals. Feeding, grooming horses for Miss Molly, that sort of thing."

"Miss Molly?"

"Ryker's daughter. She's due home this afternoon. She and her mother went to Denver on business."

Jack nodded, and handed the reins to the closest man. "I appreciate you taking care of my horse."

"That's what we do, sir. I love horses. Earning their trust, making sure they're safe. You can tell a lot about a man based on how he treats his horse."

"That so?"

The man nodded. "Yes, sir. Look at your horse, for example. He's calm and strong, like you. He knows his place, and from the way he looks at you, he trusts you and would take you anywhere without question. And judging by his strength, he's able to do so without a doubt. My guess is you can guide this horse damn near with your mind. Just a slight nudge here or there, and he knows what you need him to do."

"You get all that from looking at him?"

"And from looking at you."

"Larry, we need to get to work," the other cowboy said.

"Don't get your skirts twisted up," Larry said to his friend. "Take the horse into the pen and let him run around a bit. Me and this man are having an important conversation. I'll be back soon enough."

"We need this job, Larry."

Larry laughed. "I think we'll be working for Mrs. Ryker before the day is done. Now git."

His friend took the horse into the empty round pen.

Larry walked Jack's horse toward a line of pails stacked along the other pen. Some were filled with oats, and some with water. Jack walked with him, not knowing why.

"I read people and animals, sir," Larry said as he tied off Jack's horse to the pen. "Been doing it all my life." He moved a pail of water and a pail of oats over to the horse. He stroked the horse's face and whispered in his ear. "This is for you, boy."

The horse started drinking.

"I read people, too," Jack said.

"I know you do. I can tell by the way you carry yourself that you're a man of action, and you have a sense of right and wrong that guides you without question. One look at your right hand and your holster tells me you're a fast-draw. One look at your face tells me your aim is always spot-on."

Jack rubbed his chin.

The man held up a hand. "One look in your eyes tells me you're stalwart and true. You always aim to take the right path, no matter the danger."

"What's your point, Larry?"

"Have you met Mr. Ryker?"

"No. I've met Gus, Mondo, and the sheriff, though."

"All four of them are in the house. Nobody else in there except a housekeeper. She's an old Arapaho, and won't be any trouble to you."

"Why are you telling me this?"

"We needed the job. That's true of all the men here. But something ain't right about Mr. Ryker. He tries to come off all business-like, but his brain don't seem connected, and I think he believes he's living in one of them books he's always reading. His eyes got no soul in them."

"I don't—"

Larry shook his head. "All's I'm saying is that he's a dangerous sumbitch, and you want to shoot him first."

CHAPTER FOURTEEN

Jack knocked on the door to the main house. An ancient Indian woman opened the door.

"I'm here for Mr. Ryker," Jack said.

"He expecting you?"

Jack shook his head.

The woman nodded, and gestured for him to come inside. She pointed. "Dining room. You want eggs?"

"No thank you. I won't be here long."

She looked him up and down. "No," she said. "You won't." She pointed again. "Through there and to the left."

And she stepped outside before closing the door.

Jack stared at the door for a moment. Something told him the woman wouldn't be coming back until everything was over.

He heard voices at the back of the house in the direction the woman pointed, so he walked toward them. He passed through a room lined with bookshelves to a kitchen, and off to the left was a dining room with a sturdy table and more bookshelves surrounding it. Four men sat around the table. Mondo was the biggest; Gus was the smallest. The sheriff had his back to Jack, and seated at the head of the table was a man with long white hair. His face was grizzled and his features deep-set and powerful.

The grizzled man rose. He had piercing blue eyes that could have frozen water at a glance. "Join us, death man. I've been expecting you," he said. His voice was deep and calm.

He wore a gun on one hip and a rapier sword on the other.

Jack stepped into the room.

The sheriff turned, gun in hand.

Gus and Mondo also had guns drawn and aimed at Jack. They were all grinning.

Ryker's hands were empty. He smiled, and Jack could practically hear the sound of leather creaking as the man's face stretched. "Welcome to my humble abode," Ryker said.

"Not much of a welcome," Jack said.

"The guns are merely a precaution. If you'll remove your gun belt and place it on the floor, they will lower their weapons."

Jack's eyes swept the faces and trigger fingers. They wouldn't do anything without Ryker's approval.

Jack drew a deep breath. He might be able to shoot one or two of them, but at this range, he'd pay with his life.

He unbuckled the belt and lowered it to the floor.

The men all lowered their weapons, but did not holster them.

Ryker nodded to a corner. "There's an extra chair there. Join us."

Jack walked over and sure enough, a wooden chair stood in the corner between two bookshelves. He pulled the chair out, set it by the table and spun it so the back faced Ryker. Jack put one booted foot on the chair so he'd have easy access to his knife, and rested his hands on his knee.

"Can't say as I'm hungry," Jack said.

"Old Mrs. Skyhawk stepped outside, so there's no one to serve you anyway," Ryker said. He remained standing and faced Jack across the table.

Larry was right. Ryker needed to die first. The man commanded the room. His flowing white hair seemed unnatural, possibly because the stubble dotting his cheeks was dark black.

"Mondo here wants to fight you," Ryker said.

"He'd lose," Jack said.

"Gus here wants to challenge you to a fast-draw."

"He'd lose."

"And the sheriff wants me to simply send you away."

"There's been enough killing," the sheriff said.

"Is there ever enough killing?" Ryker asked with a wry grin.

"Some people need killing," Jack said.

"And Tombstone Jack is just the man to do it," Ryker said. "I love the nickname, by the way. Has a certain morbid ring to it. I trust there's a story that goes with the name."

"There is," Jack said, "but you'd be disappointed."

Ryker gestured at the bookshelves. They were all filled with books. "As you can tell from my library, I love stories. Have you read any of these books? You'll find a variety of wonderful titles on my shelves. Each loaded with adventure and lives we could have lived, had we only been so bold. Take a look, Jack. Do you recognize any of the titles?"

"I'm not here to talk about books."

"Of course not. But you're not the one who created the itinerary here. I did. And I want to know you before I kill you."

"I've already taken your measure, Mr. Ryker," Jack said.

"Oh, I'm sure you have, and under normal circumstances, I'm sure you'd tell me I'd come up wanting. But as I said, we're not here so you can get to know me. We're here so I can get to know you. Sheriff Dawkins said that if I wanted to kill you, the smart play was to take you out with a rifle when you first set foot on my ranch."

Jack sighed.

"Am I boring you?"

"A little."

Ryker hooks his thumbs into his belt. "Tell Sheriff Dawkins about Victor and Perry."

"They're *your* sons," Jack said. "You tell him."

Ryker smiled again, stretching his face and crinkling his eyes. He kept his gaze on Jack. "I may not be C. Auguste Dupin, but I can make some deductions of my own. Do you know Dupin?"

"I've read some Poe," Jack said.

Ryker clapped his hands. "I do so love Edgar Allan Poe," he said. "Have any of you read his work?" Ryker gestured around the table.

Mondo raised his hand. "I have."

"Really?" Sheriff Dawkins asked. "I can't imagine you reading anything."

"Now, Sheriff," Ryker said. "Don't be so quick to judge." He turned to Mondo. "What have you read?"

"Story about a murderer who heard a heartbeat under the floor. That story gave me nightmares for months."

"Ah, yes, 'The Tell-Tale Heart.' Have you read that one, Jack?"

"I have."

"And I trust you've read all three of the Dupin stories?"

Jack nodded. He kept his focus on Ryker, but also studied the others with his peripheral vision. Gus still held his gun ready to raise and fire, as did the sheriff. Mondo still held his gun, too, but he was looking more at Ryker than at Jack. He needed just a moment's distraction so he could kill Ryker, but he suspected the man was setting him up.

Ryker smiled, but it didn't reach his eyes. "Poe's detective would say that since you're standing here before us, Victor and Perry are dead."

"Dupin would be wrong," Jack said.

"Victor is a good tracker. I can't believe he wouldn't have found you."

"He was a good tracker."

"Past tense. I like it. So my son Victor is dead, but my son Perry is alive?"

"And now you're playing Dupin."

"I've always seen myself as more of an Edmond Dantès kind of man."

Jack shrugged. "Who?"

He'd read *The Count of Monte Cristo* so he knew exactly who Ryker meant, but he didn't want to give him the pleasure.

"Have you not read Dumas?"

"Perhaps you can loan me a book."

"Oh, Jack, I never loan books. People so rarely return them."

"Do you mind if I peruse your selection anyway?" Jack asked.

"Why do you want to look at his books when we're gonna kill you?" Gus asked.

"New worlds to discover," Jack said, giving Gus a wink.

Ryker glared at Gus, then gestured to the shelves. "My books are arranged alphabetical by author, so Dumas will be on that shelf behind you."

Jack turned to look at the books. Maybe he could pull one down and threaten to set it on fire. Somehow, he didn't think that would work. They'd just shoot him before he could do anything. He spotted the Dumas titles, and slid *The Three Musketeers* from the shelf.

"I liked this book," Jack said, turning.

"Do you see yourself as d'Artagnan?"

"Not really." He stepped closer to the table, but positioned himself slightly behind Sheriff Dawkins as he casually flipped a few pages in the book.

The sheriff twisted in his seat to try and keep Jack in sight.

"Who would you say most fits you in the canon of literature?"

"I'm my own man," Jack said. As he spoke, he clapped the book closed. He kicked Sheriff Dawkins' chair, driving him into the table. Dawkins' ribs cracked and he cried out.

Jack was still in motion. He threw the book at Gus. The book smacked him in the wrist, knocking the gun from his hand.

Jack dropped low, pulled his knife from his boot, and rose to let it fly. The knife plunged into Mondo's chest before the big man could even raise his gun.

Gus tried to go for his gun. Jack kicked him in the head. Ryker clapped his hands once and laughed.

"Nice moves, Jack, but you should have killed me first." As he spoke, Ryker pulled his own gun, and fired twice. The shots were aimed at an angle to avoid shooting the books should he miss.

Jack hit the ground, rolled to the gun Gus dropped, and grabbed it. He knew he should have tried for Ryker first, but it would have cost him his life as the other men already had their guns out. Gus shook his head and tried to lunge. Jack stiff-armed him backward, then shot him in the head.

Dawkins tried to get his gun, but cried out in pain when he shifted.

Jack shot him in the chest.

Dawkins collapsed.

Ryker took two more shots.

A bullet slammed into Jack's shoulder, and another grazed his neck.

He ignored the biting pain, and did a shoulder roll across the table to kick Ryker in the face.

But Ryker was too fast.

The man threw himself away from the table, and fired twice more. One shot went wide, but the other caught Jack in the chest. Jack fell to the floor in pain. Blood poured from his wounds, and the room spun.

"No!" Ryker yelled. "My books! My poor books!"

He vaulted over Jack to check the damage his bullets had done.

Jack tried to sit up, but felt consciousness go out and in. The chest wound was bad.

Ryker spun and aimed his gun at Jack's head. He pulled the trigger twice, but the gun clicked on empty chambers.

"Very well," Ryker said, tossing his gun on the table. "I'll finish you the old-fashioned way."

He drew his rapier and swished it like Edmond Dantès in the Dumas revenge novel.

"And now, Jack, it's time for you to die."

Ryker thrust the sword at Jack.

But Jack rolled to the side and the blade jammed into the floor. Jack rolled back, bending, then snapping the rapier in two with his weight.

Ryker stabbed Jack with the broken blade. It bit into his gut.

Jack grunted in pain.

He tried to punch and kick, but Ryker darted away just out of reach. Ryker danced around, rushed in and stabbed Jack in the stomach again.

"You've no way out now, Jack. You killed my son, my nephew, and my raiders, but I can get more men. You won't be getting any more blood, though. It will stain my floor, but that's what imported rugs are for. And think of the story I'll have to tell."

He stabbed Jack a third time. This one was in the chest, close to the heart.

"You should not have made me shoot my books," Ryker said. "They are my most prized possessions."

Jack tried to scoot away, leaving trails of blood in his wake.

"Trying to go someplace?" Ryker asked. "No threats about how you're going to kill me?"

Jack didn't say anything.

"All you can do now is bleed," Ryker said. "Allow me to add to your collection of puncture wounds."

He dashed in to stab Jack again, but Jack kicked Ryker's foot as it moved forward. Ryker lost his balance and fell on top of Jack.

"Time to write, *the end*," Jack said.

He grabbed Ryker's head and gave a savage twist, snapping the man's neck.

Ryker went limp. Jack shoved the body aside. It took every last bit of his strength, and as Ryker's corpse rolled off, Jack's world went dark.

CHAPTER FIFTEEN

Jack woke up in the doctor's office. Caroline stood over him.

"Welcome back," she said. "Burt has been worried about you."

"Burt brought me in?"

"No. A man named Larry, and an Indian woman brought you in. You made quite a mess out at the Ryker place. They got it all cleaned up, of course. And I got you all patched up, but you're not going anywhere for a while. New sheriff wants to talk to you, too."

Jack drew a deep breath. It hurt to breathe, but that told him he was alive. Pain wasn't much of a problem. The lack of pain would be more troublesome.

"Thanks for fixing me up," Jack said.

"It's what I do," Caroline said and patted him on the shoulder. "Shall I send Burt in?"

Jack nodded.

She left the room, and a moment later, Burt rushed in.

"You gonna make it?" Burt asked.

"Don't I always?"

"I ain't never seen you get all shot up and stabbed before."

"First time for everything, I guess."

"All the raiders are dead except Perry, who's in the jail right now. Sheriff wants to talk to you."

"So I've been told."

"Damn," Burt said. "I don't like seeing you like this."

"I'll heal."

"I know, but that ain't my point. Now that I know you're gonna make it, can I borrow some cash? Sally over at

Madam West's is calling my name. Or rather, she needs to be calling my name, but I ain't got the money to get her to do it yet."

Jack shook his head. "You never change."

"Course not. Why would I do that?"

They bantered a bit, then Burt headed out to see Sally. And a short time after that, the new sheriff dropped by.

"You remember me?" the sheriff asked.

"Should I?"

"Name's David. I was Sheriff Dawkins' main deputy."

"I believe you were going to throw me out of the station."

"That's right."

"And now you're gonna throw me in the cell next to Perry."

"You ain't leaving this office for a while, Jack. And at that point, you're free to do what you please. Mrs. Ryker

131

sends her thanks. Said her husband was off his rocker. Kept thinking he was the hero of his own book. Near as we can tell, ol' Ryker went crazy, killed his men, and tried to kill you, but fell and busted his neck. Sound about right? This is where you give me a nod."

Jack nodded.

"Very good. Thank you, sir. I'd appreciate it if you don't spend too much time in my town, though."

"I'll be moving on soon as I can."

"Excellent. Your horse is at the Ryker ranch. Man named Larry told me to tell you he's doing fine and will be ready to go when you are."

"Thanks," Jack said.

"Thank you for getting rid of old man Ryker. That man was crazy."

Jack considered that. "It's not crazy to want to be the hero of your own book. It's only crazy if you believe that gives you some divine right to kill people."

"I ain't much of a reader."

"And I'm not much for divine rights," Jack said. And with that, he faded off to sleep.

Made in the USA
Columbia, SC
06 February 2018